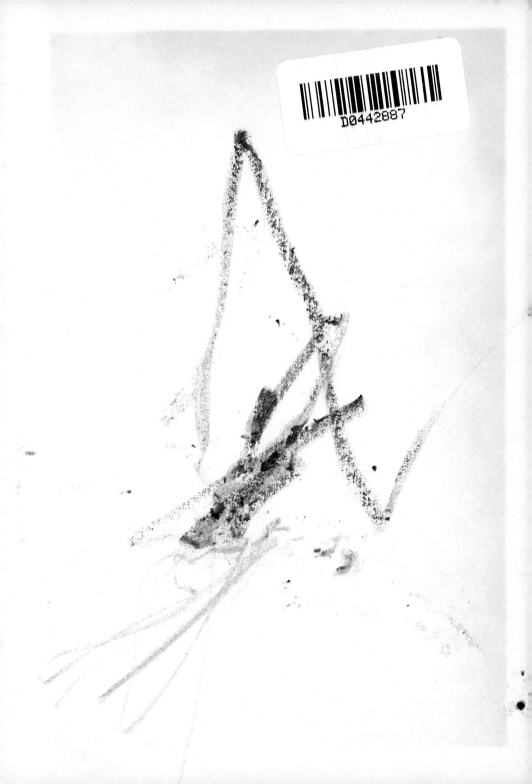

THE GINGER HORSE

Illustrated by Wesley Dennis

Weekly Reader Children's Book Club *Presents*

THE GINGER HORSE

by Maureen Daly

DODD, MEAD & COMPANY, NEW YORK

I

OUTSIDE the cottage the soft, flat light of early dawn lay against the windows like gray flannel. In the kitchen, Rob Murdoch shook the warm ashes in the old coal stove, put in two sticks of wood from the neat stack in the corner and pulled the pot of porridge from the back of the stove up over the thin blue flame.

Three crockery bowls brought from the cupboard, three spoons from the drawer and the worn wooden table was set for breakfast. It was cold in the house, cold and silent, and Rob moved slowly and quietly. Even though he was up and dressed, his face splashed clean in cold water, he was still cherishing a last few moments of feeling half asleep.

A cat meowed outside and leaped to the sill of the kitchen window, lured by the dim light and the flicker of the stove. It was a village cat, a stray, but Rob knew better than to let it in. The thick porridge on the stove, made the night before, had been measured out for three—three and no more.

At that moment, big Jock Murdoch came into the kitchen, already dressed in the rough trousers and faded plaid wool shirt he always wore for his work in the coal mines. With an irritated snap, he switched off the old china lamp on the table.

"Is the day's light not good enough for you?" he demanded loudly. "God would not have given you eyes if He didn't mean you to use them. Certainly a man doesn't need two lights to see his way around his own house. Especially a light that costs money every time it's switched on." With a big, work-roughened hand, he pushed aside the curtains at the kitchen window. The cat leaped from the sill and scuttled under an old blackberry bush.

Murdoch opened the fuel door on the iron stove, looked in at the flame and blew it into brightness with great puffs of breath, like an old bellows. "You might try to see to it that a man gets a hot breakfast on time," he said to his son. "There's no need to be daydreaming about the house when there's a day's work to be done."

"It's long before whistle-time, Father," Rob replied. "We're in no hurry yet."

"*You're* in no hurry?" his father said sharply. "You're long past twelve years old and it's *time* you got in a hurry. You'll be spending your day up at the Minister's again, with your books and your nonsense, and there'll be no need to hurry. But I've got a shift to take into the mines and a boss to account to for *my* time. And *there's* your hurry for you."

Rob stirred the slowly bubbling porridge in silence and then served up three steaming bowlfuls. He was not afraid of his

father, ever—and even loved the loud, rough sound of his voice. The brusqueness, the complaints seemed to make the house come alive. But there were times when the old man did not want to hear a human voice other than his own.

"He'd be different," Rob's older brother, Mac, had explained to him once, "if only we had a woman about. He's been afraid of the quiet ever since Mother died. And he can't even let himself think about David. Father is one of the best men in the mines but he's not good for soft talk or facing how he really feels about things. . . ."

Mac came out just then from the little bedroom he and Rob shared, smoothing back his thick, blond hair with his hand and smiling a quick good morning at his young brother. Mac was a sharp contrast to the rough bulk of his father. The older Murdoch had coarse dark hair, thickly streaked with gray, a barrel chest and a ruddy face, as lined and weathered as a sea captain's. Mac was tall, a good head taller than his father, muscular but slim, with a quick lightness in his face and manner that suggested something beyond good health and good nature. It was an alive look, the look of a man who had some wonderful inner secret that made his eyes smile and his voice quick. He had worked his first job in the mines of Duneen, Scotland, as a boy of thirteen, and even after nearly ten years in the pits, his face had none of the ingrained despair etched on the features of the older man.

The three sat at the table, heads bowed in silent prayer, while the porridge bowls sent up thin steam into the cold air. Then Jock poked at his food with his spoon, saying crustily, "You'd think there would be someone in this house who could make a man a decent dish of oatmeal."

"You made it yourself last night, Father," Mac reminded him lightly.

"And I'll thank you to keep a civil tongue in your head," the old man declared tartly, rising from the table and going to the cupboard. He took out a crock of sweet wild honey and spooned a dripping portion into each son's bowl. "Maybe that will melt a few of the lumps away," he said.

Father and sons ate in silence, contentedly, while outside the sun rose higher, banishing the mists and sending a faint rosy light into the room. The wood in the old iron stove burned with a quiet whisper.

From a far distance came the sharp, shrill blast of a whistle, two longs and two shorts, cutting through the chill morning air. It was the signal from the coal mines just outside town, calling the first shift to work, and Jock Murdoch jumped to his feet as sharply as if the whistle had called out his own name.

"You would think, wouldn't you, that a man would be allowed to finish his breakfast in peace one day in his life-time?" he said, pushing aside his bowl.

"We've a half hour yet before we're due, Father," Mac told him soothingly.

"Perhaps *you* have," Jock said, buttoning up his heavy shirt. "Perhaps you could find another job if the mines laid you off but I don't have such fancy ideas. I haven't been late a morning in thirty-odd years and I didn't hear Boss McFarlane say we were on holiday today."

Mac calmly finished his breakfast while his father waited impatiently at the half-open door.

"You know as well as I do we start the shoring up work today," the older man said. "And it will be a devil of a job getting all the pit ponies up and out of the place before we can begin the job. . . ."

"The ponies?" Rob asked eagerly.

"We won't be digging or hauling coal for about a week, I'd say," Mac explained. "He may be a tightwad, but McFar-lane knows better than to let his mines go to ruin. We'll be taking out some of the old timbers that shore up the shafts and putting in stout wood. And we'll be repairing some of the rail tracks for the coal carts. It's a lot of puffing and pulling

5

and we'll want all the pit ponies up and out of our road before we begin. McFarlane is putting the whole three dozen in his back meadow till the job is done."

"For a whole week?" Rob asked.

His brother nodded. "About that," he answered as he rose from the table. "Those poor wee horsies can stand a bit of a rest."

"There's a lot of hard-working men who wouldn't mind lazing around a week in the sun," commented Jock Murdoch, half to himself, and he stepped out the door. "And you might pull up some turnips and wash them at the pump before you get off to the Minister's," he called back to Rob. "I've left a bit of money for Mrs. McBain for a good cut of mutton for tonight. . . ."

Then the two men went off down the village street, their heavy boots sounding loud on the rough stones.

2

THE Murdoch house was set at the far end of a row of cottages on one of a dozen streets that spread out from the central square of the Scottish village, like spokes on an old wheel. Matching its neighbors, it was a small house, set close to the cobblestones, with a short bricked path leading to the front door. Behind it was a square back yard, fenced with weathered boarding and just big enough to allow room for an apple tree, some berry bushes and a patch of garden for raising turnips, cabbage, carrots and parsnips, hardy foods that would last and give a family something of its own to eat during the winter cold. Even in the snow, sturdy green cabbage plants, coarse and long-leafed, stuck up through the white cover and turnips could be spaded out of the hard ground almost all winter long. Each fall, Jock Murdoch dug up the last of his carrots and parsnips and kept them fresh by burying them in a box of coarse sand placed near the back door, all covered with heavy burlap. Just yesterday, Rob had noticed a sure sign of spring in that sand heap. The stem ends of the tough carrots he had pulled for supper were sprouting little fronds of green.

The boy stepped out now into the back garden, to dig up the turnips for which his father had asked. Then he rinsed away the earth under the garden pump. Inside once more, he carefully scraped the remains of the breakfast porridge in the three bowls into an old saucer and opened the back door again. He whistled softly and the stray tomcat, seeming to share the boy's intrigue, slipped into the kitchen, walking on silent paws. It was an old cat, with shabby, mottled fur, a squinty eye and a fight-tattered left ear. Eagerly it nibbled at the porridge, growling a little over the thick lumps, circling around the saucer as it ate, as if some enemy might snatch the food away.

Rob put the kitchen in order, set the porridge pot far back on the stove for Mrs. McBain to clean and then went into his bedroom for his school books. With a sigh, he settled down at the kitchen table for an hour of study. The old cat found himself a patch of thin sunlight on the floor and squatted down contentedly to lick the honey off his whiskers.

"The Pharaohs sent their armies up into Palestine and Syria, and conquered the peoples in these lands and made them pay tribute," Rob read aloud in a singsong voice. "Proud of their achievements, the Egyptians had their deeds in war recorded on monuments, called obelisks . . ."

Today, at the Minister's, the students of the village would study ancient life in the Valley of the Nile.

*   *   *   *

Most days seemed to have two beginnings for Rob Murdoch. The first was the gray-dawn hours before his father and brother left for the coal mines, and the second, the bright awakening when he stepped into the streets of Duneen to begin his own day.

On this late April morning, the air was still sharp and the cobblestones were slick with dew. But the sun was already brilliant over the mountains high around the village, and swirls of mist clung only to the tallest peaks or lay close to the ground in the lowest parts of the valley. Rob could smell spring in the air, the greenness of growing things and the dampness of flowing water that had been locked up so long in winter ice. It was a day made for running and shouting, for dashing up the mountainside to climb steep rocks and leap rushing streams, but instead Rob set off soberly down the street, his schoolbooks, held by a heavy leather strap, swinging close to his ankles.

It was a serious business to be a student at the Minister's. Most of the boys Rob's age, or only a little older, were already working full-time in the coal mines or serving as apprentices with the garage man, the shoemaker, the butcher or in any one of the dozen small shops in town. To study beyond the sixth year of school seemed to many of the older folk of Duneen, such as Jock Murdoch, a bold and useless thing to do. Mac Murdoch had left the village school and gone into the mines at thirteen and his brother David when he was only twelve.

Old Jock Murdoch himself had worked a lifetime in the mines, for he firmly believed that a man was *made* for work and that a man should thank God that there was work to be *done*. He also believed—and voiced those beliefs often and loudly—that a boy was raised to help out his family, and once he had learned to read and write, there was no use to study a lot more nonsense that would never do him any good. But Rob's mother had wanted him to continue at school and that outweighed his own beliefs with Jock Murdoch.

In the village of Duneen, beautiful but poor, set in its own valley and ringed off from the rest of Scotland by a wall of rugged mountains, there was but one main industry, one way for most men to earn their keep—the coal mines. That weekly pay envelope seemed to Jock Murdoch like the fountainhead of life. Many in the village thought like him. Therefore it was mostly the girls of Duneen who were allowed to "waste time" at the Minister's.

Rob hummed as he walked along, trying resolutely to re-mind himself how lucky he was to be going to sit in a class-room on this bright and blowy spring morning. Trout would be biting in the mountain streams, he knew, on a fine day like this. . . .

At the end of the street, Rob stopped at a cottage gate and gave a low, whistling signal. It was the McBain house, small and simple, but somehow different from the others in the row. On each side of the doorway stood a wooden tub, empty now but colorful with flowers all summer long, and the two small front windows were crisscrossed with light yellow curtains, fringed with heavy white cotton lace. The door itself was bright blue.

Rob had been in that house many times and always marveled at what the touch of a woman's hand could do. On the parlor side of the main room, each chair had a tatted doily on its back and on a carved wooden pedestal stood a big, drooping fern, as fresh and alive as a green fountain. There was also a blue painted table and a strip of speckled linoleum on the floor of the kitchen half of the room, and a big circle of woven rag-rug on the parlor side. Even the sewing machine had its own bright cover of blue velvet, embroidered all over with violets in thick, shaded wool.

Mrs. McBain was a young, good-looking woman, warm-hearted but strong and she had succeeded in supporting this cottage as her own home, even though her husband had been killed in a mine accident nearly ten years ago. Sarah McBain took in sewing for the village and managed to make enough money to keep life together for herself and her only child, Katie McBain. And for an hour or so every day, always when the men were at work, she slipped down to the Murdoch house to sweep, dust and put things in order. When she left, the cottage was neat and some kind of supper—lamb stew or perhaps potatoes with sausage—was set to simmer on the stove. Old Jock allowed just so much money for each meal but Mrs. McBain made it stretch far.

Once in a while, without a word to anyone, she would fix a steamed suet pudding, filled with gooseberry jam from her own shelves, or put together the dough for Scottish *scones*, filling the bread-stuff with sliced apples, butter and sugar that would melt and sputter into thick juice when the *scones* were cooked that evening on an old iron griddle. Jock Murdoch always complained about the extravagances of such food, even though he was perfectly willing to watch the *scones* cook and turn them carefully himself, like great pancakes.

So in and out of the Murdoch house Mrs. McBain went like a bright ghost. Because of the strictness of village life, she never came when the older men were at home, seeing Mac and his father only at Sunday church, to exchange formal greetings, never suggesting by word or look that she had ironed the white shirts they wore or that a carefully patched jacket might be her own handiwork.

But Sarah McBain was like a part-time mother to young Rob, blowing him a good-by kiss from the doorway on a school morning, or inviting him in for a cup of tea on a blustering, snowy afternoon after a day in the chilly classrooms at the Minister's.

Rob whistled again and swung the McBains' creaking gate to let Katie know he was waiting. In a moment, she hurried out the door, holding her books in one hand and trying to pull on a thick cardigan over her dark blue dress with the other.

"I'm late," she said apologetically, "because Mother's been putting ribbons in my hair." She turned her head to show him the long, thick braid that hung between her shoulders, inter-twined all the way with a shiny, red ribbon.

"There were some bits left from the trimmings she's put on a dress for Mrs. McFarlane," Katie explained, "and Mother

sewed them together to twist in my braid."

"It's a pretty thing she did," Rob admitted, his voice gruff with sudden embarrassment. Then he started off toward school with big steps, barely waiting for Katie to keep up with him.

Since early childhood, Katie and Rob had been closest friends, sitting side by side in class, going to the village square together on Market Day and climbing the rocks and exploring the mountains on holidays. Katie had always been a tomboy, small, wiry and fast as a rabbit. Just a few months younger than Rob, she had taken a fierce pride in keeping apace with him, following him up the slipperiest mountain trails or climbing out onto the narrowest ledge of rock. Lately, as she neared her teens, Katie had developed a new respect, a kind of shyness, for Rob. She had begun to feel that, as a boy, he was truly stronger, faster and wiser and she respected him for this. Now she hurried her steps on the damp cobblestones to keep up with him.

"I've two rye buns with jam in my pocket for lunch," she confided. "The plum jam one is for you."

"And I've brought an extra apple for you," Rob told her. "The Minister will probably let us eat in the graveyard today, if the sun keeps up. It could be warm enough to go without sweaters by noontime."

From some distance away, a church bell began to toll and both children broke into a run. "We don't want to be kept after class at the Minister's today of all days," Rob called over his shoulder. "Do hurry a bit. My brother says all the pit ponies are to be rounded up in McFarlane's meadow today. I was even hoping the Minister would let us out a bit early this afternoon."

3

THE classroom at the Minister's was not really a classroom at all but a long, damp corridor-like area that ran along the back of the old church, built on a half-century ago to hold dusty hymnbooks, birth, death and marriage records and whatever overflow of paraphernalia came from the religious life of the parish. Up to the sixth grade, the children of Duneen could go to the regular village school. The Minister himself had set up extra classes when he was first sent down from the big city of Edinburgh, some ten years ago, using old church pews as school benches and two long tables as desks.

It was just the past September that Rob and Katie had first slipped into one end of a school pew at the Minister's.

The schoolroom backed up directly into the old graveyard, a straggling, moss-slick scramble of aging headstones, wooden crosses and stone angels made chipped and blunt-nosed by the cracking frosts of Scottish winters. In cold weather, this class-room was chill as the old church itself and the fat little stove which the Minister kept stoked with coal never gave out more than a brief ring of heat. In winter, the girls sat nearest the stove and the boys shivered and swung their legs to keep their feet off the solid, aching cold of the stone floor.

Today, with the sun already casting shadows from the head-stones, the Minister threw open the classroom door, letting some of the spring warmth blow into the room. With it came the sound of birds and the whisper of wind in the new leaves of the ivy vines that blanketed the back of the church. And the warm, earth-scented breeze seemed to make a restless stir among the students, like a strong draft in a chicken coop.

The Minister rapped the edge of his desk with a ruler. "Students," he said quietly, "we'll do what we've got to do today and we'll do it as good students." His precise teacher's voice was softened by the warm tones of his Edinburgh accent. "If the recitations go well this morning, we'll *all* slip down to McFarlane's at noontime to watch the ponies come in." The thin, sensitive face was grave as he spoke but his eyes were as excited and alight as those of the students before him.

It's so like the Minister, Rob thought to himself admiringly. It's so like him to know what we're thinking and wanting to do, and say it's all right. My father would complain; he'd com-plain that it's all nonsense to study and it's all nonsense to want to see the horses, but the Minister thinks a little of both is a good thing.

There was the sound of the ruler being tapped once again,

then the Minister twirled the old globe of the world on his desk and stopped it at Egypt with a flat thumb. The morning's work began.

*　　*　　*　　*

At high noon, the class was dismissed and the students filed quietly to the schoolroom door, then burst out into the sunlight to rush over the slippery paths of the graveyard and on through the wide grove of aspen trees that separated the church property from the McFarlane meadow. The Minister followed behind, walking with Katie, and swinging his shabby black jacket like a school boy on holiday.

The meadow and the long, fenced paddock lay directly behind Angus McFarlane's big house. Three sides of the paddock were made of split-rail fencing and the fourth side was sealed off by a five-foot stone wall that backed the McFarlane garden. The house, lived in by the owner of the coal mines—and his father and grandfather before him—was the biggest one in the village, a porched and turreted structure of wood, repainted every second year in a dull, pompous red. The many windows were shrouded with white lacy curtains and the front yard was shut off from the street by a fence of pointed black iron. It was a proud house and a secret house where almost no one called except a visitor or two from Glasgow or Edinburgh, and the Minister himself. The McFarlanes had no children but there was probably not a child in the village of Duneen who had not, at one time or another, been boosted up to peek over the high back wall.

Inside, there was a garden to see! To all of Duneen, the McFarlanes seemed rich—rich and different—and theirs was a garden that grew only fruits and flowers. It had little white benches for sitting, a round stone water basin for birds and strawberry beds that grew berries as big as wild plums. In the winter months, those strawberry patches were bedded down under heavy straw, tucked in against the cold as carefully as a pampered child. Mrs. McFarlane was proud of that garden.

Around the paddock, school children and villagers milled now, laughing and talking like a crowd at a county fair. Rob had saved a place at the railing for Katie and the Minister, and they leaned against the rough wood, feeling the sun warm and soothing on their shoulders. Katie brought out the rye buns and Rob offered an apple to the Minister. Together, they munched in contented silence, waiting for the ponies to come.

*   *   *   *

Suddenly, from the far end of the paddock, there came a shout and a drumming of hoofs. Old McFarlane himself appeared, looking hot and dusty in a stiff black business suit. He swung open the corral gate and stepped aside as the first of the little pit ponies trotted up the steep path from the mine shed and ran out into the meadow. He was followed by about two dozen more ponies at a fast run that tore at the turf and raised a cloud of dust behind them. They were herded by two old collie dogs, running back and forth and nipping at the ponies' hoofs until the little animals entered into the meadow corral as neatly as a pack of docile sheep.

Katie gave a cry of delight. "They are so *small*," she exclaimed. "So lovely and small!"

For a few moments the Shetlands stood in a knot, just inside the gate, dazed by the noise of the crowd and blinking into the strange sunlight. Most of the ponies were only slightly over three feet tall, short in the leg, but stocky and wide in the body, sturdy and thick with muscle. Some were a dark, smoky black, with full heavy manes and tails of gray. Others looked almost reddish, but most of the Shetlands were a flat brown, dusted over with a layer of coal dust. Long, full tails swung almost to the ground and the heavy manes hung over the crest of the back and down the forehead in a thick fringe that almost covered the eyes. The small band of animals seemed to be staring out at the villagers and the bright, sunlit world in a mood of bewilderment.

"Poor wee beasts," said the Minister softly. "Some of them

haven't been out of the pits or the mine shed in their lifetime."

But suddenly, as if by a secret signal, a half-dozen ponies broke from the group and began a wild dash around the paddock, running, leaping and kicking their heels so high that clods of earth flew into the air. Others joined the chase, stretching their short legs to run with a sharp clip-clop that filled the spring air with sound and the fresh scent of torn-up grass and damp sod. Except for a few older ponies and a couple of mares that stood near the gate with their spindly-legged foals, the meadow was suddenly milling with the wild and excited antics of the Shetlands. The crowd lined up along the fences started to laugh and some began to clap their hands out of sheer pleasure at the sight.

Rob felt his heart pound with excitement and he hoisted himself up to sit on the top rail of the fence. Many times he had seen cows or herds of sheep driven into town on market day. And often, in the silence of the mountains, he had glimpsed roe deer and watched pine martens leaping among the trees, but never had he seen such a scene of sheer animal exuberance and hoof-skittering joy. In the brilliance of the day and the softness of the breeze, he felt his own feet want to run and jump. He had the sudden happy conviction that he knew just how the Shetlands must feel.

"Do you think they *know* they're out of the mines?" he asked the Minister. "I mean, do you think they wonder why they're not down there in the dark, pulling coal carts along the track?"

The Minister laughed understandingly. "Look at that one

over there, the one rolling on his back. He knows at least that the grass is cool and fresh!" The little pony was tossing from side to side, kicking at the air with his sharp hoofs.

"My brother Mac told me these ponies are stronger than mules," Rob said with awe. "The miners can load a half-ton of coal in a cart and a Shetland can still pull it himself. Just say, 'Gee-up, laddie,' and away he goes, right back to the entrance of the mine where they load the coal on the train. And going back and forth in the tunnels, one of these ponies can walk twenty miles a day or more."

The Minister nodded in agreement. "They're sturdy beasts and they're quick on their feet. Years ago, as a young lad, I visited the Shetland Islands, way off the northern coast of Scotland, you know. It's a barren place and rocky, with little for men to live on, let alone animals. But that's where the Shetlands come from and the breed is as sure-footed as goats and can find a bit of grass here, a bit of grass there to eat—just like a goat."

"They must be frightened, Minister, down in the dark of the coal mines," Katie said in a small voice. "I'd be out of my head with fright myself."

By now, some of the ponies seemed to have run themselves tired and, except for a high-spirited few, the meadow became quiet. Several animals drank thirstily from the little stream that ran through the paddock, while others nibbled calmly at the short grass. The two old collies settled down in a spot of shade and, one by one, the villagers began to drift back toward town. The Minister said good-by and went off through the aspen grove to the church. The Shetland that had been rolling and kicking its feet in the air was now pawing the ground and shaking its mane, bounding back and forth like a playful dog. The damp grass had ruffed up its mane and wiped much of the coal dust from its coat, which showed through the color of rich ginger. The pony's kicking and cavorting brought it near to the fence where the children stood.

Rob remembered the single apple left in his pocket.

"Ginger!" he called softly. "Here little ginger horse!" Then he held out the apple, setting it carefully on the palm of his open hand. The pony stopped and started toward the fence, his soft, brown eyes alert and watchful through the strands of mane. "Come on, Ginger, be a friend," Rob urged in a quiet voice. The pony moved closer to the fence. He was a squat, very broad-shouldered Shetland, rough, wild and untidy with a tomboy look about him, but he kept his bright, soft eyes on Rob. Finally, he planted his short front legs solidly on the turf and stretched his neck out until the apple was just within grasp of the square, white teeth. He took it carefully, then, in a flash, whirled and dashed to the other side of the paddock.

From behind Katie and Rob sounded a sudden, angry shout. "Do you not have a wit in your head, Rob Murdoch? Do you not know that some of those ponies have the temper of the devil and would like as not nip the hand off your arm?" It was big Angus McFarlane, towering over them in his black suit, his face almost as red as the red bristles of his hair.

"I was just giving my apple to the wee one there," Rob explained, gesturing to the other side of the pasture.

"And you'll be having the lot of them so spoiled they'll be

wanting apples and petting for the rest of their lives," the man declared, staring sternly down at them.

"It was my apple," Rob said firmly.

"And it's *my* pony and it's *my* land you're on!" McFarlane roared out. "And if you don't have anything better to do than moon around, I'll speak to your father about finding a place for you in the mines. A bit of hard work might teach you some manners."

"Yes, sir," Rob said, feeling the blood rushing into his cheeks. Katie was staring hard at the ground, hands jammed in the pockets of her sweater, looking as if she might cry. "We're off for home now, Mr. McFarlane," the boy said, and the two children began to walk slowly back to the village.

4

BEHIND them, off below the sprawling sheds and coal heaps of the mines, Katie and Rob heard the clear *toot-toot* and then the churning *chug-chug* of the freight train leaving on its daily trip out of the valley, through the mountain tunnels and on to the big city of Edinburgh, more than a hundred miles away. There the coal would be unloaded, to be used in factories or shipped out in great freighters to industrial centers around the world. Each afternoon that train went out on the single track . . . and each pre-dawn morning it chugged back into Duneen, its open coal-cars ready to take on the day's load.

Ever since he was a little boy, Rob had loved the sound of that whistle and engine. It had always seemed to him a brave and adventurous train to churn its way through the mountain passes into the outside world. But today, with the echo of McFarlane's rage hanging over him like a cloud of shame, even the bright toot of the whistle could not make him smile. It was bad enough to be afraid of Mr. McFarlane, but to be afraid in front of Katie was nearly unbearable. Most of the sunlight seemed to have gone out of the afternoon.

"I'm to stop at the bakery," Katie said when they reached the village square. "Mother said to bring home a fresh loaf for our supper."

"I'll go on without you then," Rob said, kicking at a cobblestone with the toe of his boot. "I have some work with my books I can do before the sun goes down." Katie nodded in understanding and said nothing.

The little bakery, with its small plate-glass window crisscrossed by white curtains, was owned by the Burns family. It was clean, neat and filled with the odors of pastry and spice. The whole Burns family worked here, father and son making the bread and cakes in the big back kitchen, mother and daughter tending shop over the worn marble counter in front.

Margaret Burns was twenty, slim and strong, with skin as fair as cake frosting and thick red hair that smelled faintly of vanilla. She was a favorite with the village children because she could always find a broken cookie or some scraps of candy at the bottom of a jar for those who stopped by "just to look," without a penny to spend. But for a reason that Rob could not clearly explain, even to himself, he no longer felt quite right about stopping at the bakery.

For about a year now, Margaret Burns had been Mac Murdoch's best girl. Nothing was said yet about marriage but they walked together on Sundays, occasionally went on picnics in the mountains or sat side by side in church. And the friendship made old Jock Murdoch angry. Not that he minded the walks and the picnics, he would not even have minded a marriage. But he did mind the studying Mac did at the bakery.

The baking at the Burns' was done late at night, so the bread and buns would be fresh for the earliest shopper in Duneen in the morning. From ten until long after midnight, the big bakery kitchen was lighted and busy, with ovens fired, bread dough rising under clean, white sheets and both Burns men working in a haze of flour dust. And on a chair in the corner, his books on his knees, Mac Murdoch would sit studying, oblivious to the work going on around him.

At first he had studied at home, having sent to Edinburgh for a set of books on drafting. He liked the devising, measuring and figuring, the drawing of neat, precise plans on fresh paper. But the sight of the young man at work had stirred up old Jock.

"You'll not sit up ruining your eyes and wasting the light in my house," he scolded, stomping about the small Murdoch kitchen. "You've *got* your job, haven't you? What are you dreaming and scheming for something else for?"

In the beginning, Mac had tried to reason with his father, explaining that by studying he might make himself fit for something besides a lifetime in the darkness of the coal pits, but talk only seemed to make the old man more upset. Many nights, Rob had huddled in his bed, a pillow over his head, while the two ranted and stormed about the kitchen.

"The valley's not good enough for you, is that it?" the older man would shout in a voice tight with frustration and rage.

"You're ashamed of the village and you're ashamed of the mines, isn't that right?" Sometimes his bitter anger soared until Rob was afraid he might strike Mac or shove his books into the iron stove.

One night, Jock Murdoch had almost sobbed. "You want to go, too, don't you? You want to leave your own village. You're determined to have your own way, aren't you? Is it not enough that I have one son dead because he wouldn't abide by the life the Lord laid out for him?"

"Our David did what he had to do," Mac said quietly. "Even if he died, Father, he wasn't afraid to live."

"He disobeyed me and he's dead," Jock Murdoch said numbly, staring down at the back of his thick, work-roughened hands.

Mac gathered his papers and sketches into a neat pile on the kitchen table and said gently, "If my books bother you so much, Father, you'll see them no more."

And from that night on, Mac did his studying at the bakery, coming back after midnight, closing the door carefully behind him, even though he sensed his father was still wide awake, brooding and staring up at the ceiling in his chill, lonesome bedroom.

Except for that one emotional night, young Rob had never heard his father mention his brother's name since his death. But that very silence and despair had kept David Murdoch very much alive in the house.

His photograph, showing a slight, dark-haired young man in a Royal Air Force uniform, and a pair of bronze wings, sent back to Duneen after David's death at the war front, were kept carefully wrapped in an old shirt in Rob's bottom bedroom chest drawer.

"Our David just ran away, you know," Mac had explained to Rob several years ago. "He wasn't made for the mines and he just couldn't take it anymore. It was only a few months before you were born and I think he felt that, with a new child in the house, Father might forgive him. One afternoon, he slipped out on the coal train and the next thing we knew, a letter arrived from Edinburgh. He wrote once a week all those months he was in training, but he must have been afraid to come home, even on leave. And then he shipped out to the war front, and we never saw him again. When the official notice came after his death, Father just seemed to turn into an old man overnight. He burned David's letters, put his picture away and never said his name again. Mother's lungs had always been bad, but after David's death she was worse. And when she died, Father felt her loss was part and parcel of the whole thing.

"You were too small and I was all he had left to talk to, yet he couldn't seem to talk to me. He's still hurt and angry and he thinks he'll never forgive David for running away . . . but I think he's never really forgiven himself for making him go."

So Rob's heart ached for a hero brother he had never seen, but out of stubborn loyalty to his father, he kept away from the bakery. He was puzzled somewhat by his own feelings, disturbed by the idea that perhaps his father was wrong, yet still he kept away.

The Murdoch house was silent but warm and alive with the

smell of a mutton stew, simmering slowly on the stove when Rob reached home. He looked into the iron pot and his mouth watered at the sight of the chunk of gray meat, the pinkish turnips and the big, mealy potatoes, cooking slowly and thickening the gravy. Dutifully, he put his schoolbooks in the bedroom and began to set the table for supper.

On the stroke of five, the two Murdoch men tramped down the street, into the house and out to the back garden. Stripping to the waist, they washed off at the garden pump, lathering their faces and arms with yellow soap, sluicing away the suds with cold water and then stomping around to keep warm as they waved their arms in the air to dry. The mountain winds were still touched with chill.

The mood of the supper table was lifted by the tenderness of the mutton and the reviving nourishment of the vegetables. Each full plate seemed to be haloed in its own steam. Rob ate in silence for a few moments, then began to think with renewed excitement of the pleasures of the afternoon.

In a quick, animated voice, he began to tell his father and brother about the antics of the ponies. His tone was breathless as he recounted the running, jumping and spinning about of the little Shetlands. In the end, he even told them about the ginger horse and his own run-in with Mr. McFarlane.

"Just a blathering old windbag," said Mac calmly, mopping up some thick gravy with a bit of potato. "He's got nothing to say and he says it all day long at the top of his voice."

Jock Murdoch slapped the table firmly with the flat of his hand. "You'll not talk like that in my house," he said sternly.

"You've no right to call names on the very man who gives you your bread and butter."

"That's just it, Father," Rob said eagerly. "Why *does* Mr. McFarlane care if I give the ginger pony an apple? He's *got* all the bread and butter in the world. He's *got* the mines and a big house and owns half the village . . . almost. He's got so much. And the pony *liked* me. And the thing is, Father, it's such a wee little horse—." Rob's voice broke off suddenly and he knew, to his dismay, that if he said another word, he would cry.

His father looked at him strangely for a moment, then asked gruffly, "And who says Boss McFarlane has everything when he's got not a chick nor child to share it with? He doesn't know all there is to know about life, with all his big house. You didn't see that wee ginger horse trying to make friends with *him*, did you?" Jock Murdoch snorted and went back to eating his stew.

Rob kept his tear-bright eyes down on his own plate. Whatever is the matter with me, he thought. Now I want to cry again.

5

THE next morning Rob left earlier than usual for the Minister's. But first he stepped into the back yard to pull two carrots out of the sandpile. "It's not as if I were stealing from Father," he told himself. "I'll just not eat my share next time we have carrots for supper."

With Katie, Rob short-cutted around the McFarlane house and out to the meadow. The morning was quiet and the little ponies seemed subdued and content in the mellow sunlight. The children spotted the ginger horse at one side of the fence and ran toward him. The Shetland started and skittered away. Rob held out a carrot and walked slowly along the fence line, calling softly, "Here, Ginger. Come on, Ginger!" The little animal watched him, bright eyes staring cautiously through his heavy mane, backing away at each step the boy took. He seemed to have forgotten yesterday.

"We might try him again after classes," Katie suggested

soothingly. "He's probably been up with the sun and has had his fill of grass already."

In mid-afternoon, the children came back again. The ginger horse was standing in the brook, looking down at the cold water swirling around its fetlocks.

"Perhaps if we just stand quiet, he might come to us," Rob said, leaning against the fence.

This time, the pony seemed to know the boy and girl were there. His ears pricked, his tail switched and he held his head up, as if listening into the wind. Beside him, Rob felt Katie shiver with excitement.

Suddenly, the ginger horse bolted from the brook and began a fast caper around the field, nipping now and then at other ponies until a half dozen had joined the run. The Shetland skipped and turned, like someone inventing a fast game of follow-the-leader. Then he stopped abruptly, skidding to a halt with his front legs stiffened against the ground. With a shake of his mane, he began rolling on the grass, legs in the air, tossing from side to side.

"I think he's showing off," Rob exclaimed with wonder. "I really believe that pony is showing off."

"I'll try him again," Rob said when the Shetland was standing quiet once more, and he called out, "Hi, there, Ginger! I've got something for you!"

The pony trotted cockily up near the fence, stood again just as far away as his short neck would reach and took the carrot from Rob's hand. Still watching the children, he backed away a few steps and munched on the carrot. Rob held out the second one, and the pony went through the same little ceremony of coming fairly close, taking it and backing up. His eyes never seemed to leave the children's faces, as if he were watching and testing their friendship.

The next day, Rob brought two more carrots from the Murdoch sand heap. By the middle of the week, the ginger horse seemed as responsive as a friendly kitten. On each visit he seemed to put on his own kind of show for the children, running, jumping and cavorting, and then coming docilely to the fence for a carrot. At last, he moved close enough so that Rob could reach out and touch his coarse blond mane, brushing aside the long hairs until the soft brown eyes were clearly visible. Four days in the clean grass of the meadow and the water of the brook had washed the coal dust off the light red-brown coat, and spring winds had fluffed the mane until it lay over the pony's crest like a big shawl. The little animal stood patiently, but apprehensively, while the children patted him and then, as if embarrassed by his own affection, darted away.

On Thursday morning, Rob searched the sandpile for two small, wizened carrots. Then, guiltily, he kicked at the sand to make it look more plump and filled. Again that day the little horse romped and played for his treat.

At supper that evening, Rob spoke to his father. "I thought I'd be eating fewer carrots in the next few weeks, Father," he said haltingly .

"And are you now getting finicky about your food, instead

34

of thanking God each day that you've *got* a bite to eat?" his father demanded crossly.

"It's not that, Father," confessed Rob. "I've been feeding some of our carrots to McFarlane's little Shetland I told you about. . . ."

Old Jock Murdoch put down his fork and stared at the boy. His voice was puzzled. "Do you not think you've gone a bit daft over that wee pony? You'll be bringing it sugar buns next, or a pillow to sleep on. It's not like it's yours to keep. By Saturday noon, that pony and the rest of them will be back in the mines where they belong. . . ."

"*By Saturday noon?*" Rob asked.

"They'll be rounded up and back in before the noon whistle," his brother Mac explained. "We work just half days on Saturdays, as you know, and McFarlane wants the mines in order and working full tilt by Monday morning."

Rob felt his cheeks flush with color but his lips seemed too pale and stiff to speak. He felt his father's eyes on his face.

"Take what old carrots you like, lad," Mr. Murdoch said kindly. "I'd rather eat parsnips myself, or better something green, if I had my choice."

Late on Friday afternoon, Rob and Katie clung to the paddock fence once more, watching the little pony, feeding him—and holding back one carrot to the very last.

"Do you think we might ever go down to the mines to see him?" Katie asked.

"You know well how Mr. McFarlane is about children hanging around the coal pits," Rob answered.

"Perhaps just once he'd let us go, if your brother Mac asked him?" she suggested hopefully.

"Never," Rob said with sad conviction. "Mr. McFarlane is not that kind of a man."

The sun was beginning to set, showing pink and purple on the high tips of the mountains and lighting the valley with a last show of gold light. Behind the church, starlings were twittering in the aspen grove, flitting from tree to tree with the busy excitement that seems to touch birds just before sundown. The whole valley of Duneen was coming to rest, a flat, green saucer set within the cup of the mountains.

Katie looked at Rob. "We're nearly late for our supper now," she said.

For the last time, Rob called out to the ginger pony. He trotted close to the fence, took the carrot and stood his ground, eating noisily and happily, while Rob stroked the blond mane. Then the boy cupped the pony's soft, warm muzzle in the palm of his hand and laid his cheek against the tawny forehead.

"I think," he said sadly, "you're the most beautiful wee beast that ever lived on earth."

*   *   *   *

Saturday was market day in Duneen, a crowded, bustling day of shopping, gossiping and getting in supplies for the following week. From early morning until long after dark, the little village had a festive air. Crofters from the small farms tucked here and there at the base of the mountains drove their sheep into town, the tinkling bells on the lead ewes echoing out over the valley. The bleat and baas of the woolly animals made a special Saturday music in Duneen. Old farm women tramped into the village to sell a bit of home produce in the town square —a pair of ducks, a basket of fresh eggs, wild plum jam or jars of honey collected from hives on the sunnier slopes of the mountains.

On market day, most of the shops of Duneen put special counters right out on the sidewalk to attract buyers. Stewart, the dry goods merchant, laid out bolts of wool cloth, white netting for parlor curtains and baskets filled with bright skeins of wool. The hardware store displayed cookie jars, mixing bowls and pots and pans that glinted in the sun. Jaimie Lauder, the town butcher, had a special offering of haggis, a kind of oatmeal-and-liver-stuffed sausage, in his window and he festooned his doorway with a trio of blown-up sheeps' bladders that floated up like a bunch of little white balloons to mark his shop for the crowd. Around the bakery, the air was sweet with the "Saturday special," little gingerbread cakes filled with candied fruit and baked in cups of pleated paper. And on the doorstep of the shop, old Granny Merkle took her customary Saturday place, hawking small baskets of brown mushrooms that she grew in her own cellar.

Saturday sounds and smells were everywhere. Old Thomas the Tinker drove his shabby green horse-wagon with its little stove and grindstone to one side of the square. His wife sat up on the driver's seat, banging an old wash tub and calling out, "Knives sharpened! Pots mended! Come round, come round— the tinker's in town!" At the fish-and-chips stall, at the far cor-

ner of the square, a tub of sputtering hot lard sent blue smoke and mouth-watering smells into the air, as thick slices of potatoes and squares of whitefish were dropped into the fat to fry crisp. For only a few pennies one could buy a snack of fish and chips, served in a cone of brown paper and flavored with a dash of vinegar.

Even the village tavern, called The Old Ram's Head, opened its swinging doors at six on market day mornings. All day, except in the warmest weather, a bit of fire sputtered in the hearth and farmers and villagers stopped by for a drop of cheer. With the fine April weather warming the valley, this promised to be a good Saturday for Duneen.

Rob tidied the house when the menfolk left for their half-day in the mines. He pulled up the covers on the three narrow beds, sprinkled a little sand on the kitchen floor to catch the dust and then swept it clean. Just an hour before noon, he put on his best brown sweater, tucked into his pocket the shiny farthing piece Mac had given him to spend and set off for the square with Katie. Together, they pushed through the village streets, jostled about in the market crowd, stopping to price this and admire that. They both knew they were really heading for the paddock, to see the ponies rounded up, but neither wanted to be the first to mention the sad affair.

By loitering, by pretending to be absorbed in the sights of market day, they reached the McFarlane meadow just as old McFarlane himself arrived in view with three miners, all carrying stout sticks, and the familiar pair of collie dogs trotting behind.

McFarlane stood at the gate, gesturing and shouting. "Stand back all of you," he bellowed at the crowd of villagers and country folk who lined the fences. "What are you gaping at? Have you never seen a pony in your lives? We haven't all day to do a simple job."

The collies slipped under the fence and began to circle the field, shifting and moving, rounding the ponies up toward the gate. "We'll take them out in sixes," McFarlane said to the miners. "In that way, we'll get them back in good order, without a jam-up at the sheds."

He swung open the paddock gate and waited while the dogs herded five ponies and a tiny colt out through the opening and onto the road leading to the mines. McFarlane clicked the gate shut. Most of the other Shetlands then milled up to the gate, pawing and whinnying, seemingly eager to get back to their old underground stalls. A few minutes later, the gate was opened again and a half-dozen more ponies trotted docilely out of the pasture.

Rob looked out over the field, trying to spot the ginger horse among the moving ponies. When he finally saw him, he put his hand on Katie's arm. "Look at that, will you, Katie!" he cried in astonishment.

Near the far end of the meadow, the little Shetland was alone, standing in the brook, bending down his muzzle to drink, then lifting his head to shake the water drops off his mane in a rhythmic kind of game. He was paying no attention to the other ponies, the collies or the shouts of McFarlane.

Group by group, the ponies were guided from the field until there were just five left—and the ginger horse day-dreaming in the brook. The collies herded the five toward the gate, then headed out at a trot toward the single horse. He saw them coming and shook his mane with a kind of impatience. Then, quick as a deer, he leaped from the shallow water, ran between the two dogs and straight at the pack of ponies near the gate. First they scattered in fright and then, caught up with the sudden action, pounded around the field after the ginger horse, making a small thunder with their rapid hoofs.

Patiently, the old, well-trained collies circled among the ponies, nipping a heel here, barking there, rounding them up in a tighter circle as the animals tired, herding them once more toward the gate. But the ginger horse skittered to one corner of the paddock and stood with his tail to the fence.

"Get the five out of here," McFarlane called in exasperation, "and then I'll attend to that devil." He shook his fist in the direction of the pasture. Five ponies, heaving and panting, were let out the gate and down the pathway to the pits.

Rob felt his heart pounding in excitement, and the wood of the fence was harsh under the tight grasp of his hands. McFarlane whistled the dogs back into the meadow, then said softly, "Get him, lads."

The dogs trotted off across the meadow, then approached the pony slowly, with tails wagging and manner friendly, coming in one from each side, doing a familiar job like the good herders they were. But they might as well have tried to corner a bit of ginger brown lightning. In a flash, the pony was out of the corner and bounding about the meadow, running at a rapid clip, switching and changing courses, with the dogs close behind. For more than five minutes, the little Shetland twisted and turned, while the old collies panted, circled and tried to close in. The pony was breathing hard now, his ribs rising and falling. A fleck of foam showed on his muzzle. For a moment he stood stiff and still in the middle of the meadow. One dog stalked slowly up in front, the other circled behind. The crowd was strangely silent, as if watching a deadly game. Then the pony snapped alive, kicked out with a hind leg and caught one old dog a glancing blow on the side of the head, tossing it squealing onto its back. The ginger horse bounded, panting, to the other side of the meadow. The injured dog ran yipping from the field, with its companion whimpering and scampering behind.

From McFarlane there came a roar of indignation. "Get me a rope," he shouted. "We'll show this hot-tempered devil who's boss in this village!" One of the miners handed him a length of stout rope which the mine owner fashioned into a lasso. "Come on with your sticks," he said to the three miners. "Drive him into a corner and I'll get this over his blathering head."

The pony stood firm, watching warily as the four men walked toward him over the sunlit grass. When they were about six feet away, he charged around them and back across the field. Again they approached, again he twisted away from them. The more the men shouted, the faster they tried to run at him, the quicker the Shetland skittered away.

Mr. McFarlane's beefy face turned a sullen red. He wiped his hot forehead with a pocket handkerchief. "Give me your stick," he said to one of the miners. "This is a beastie that needs a lesson he will never forget."

"No, no, Mr. McFarlane!" Rob called out, his voice bursting from his throat. "You can't! You can't! The wee pony doesn't think like you do. He just wants to be out. He doesn't want to go back in the mines. He doesn't want to be a pit pony any more. . . ."

With a leap, the boy vaulted the fence and ran toward the older man, shouting and waving his arms. He had no plan, no idea what he meant to do. He only knew he could not let Mr. McFarlane lay a stick on the beautiful ginger pony.

McFarlane stopped short with astonishment and turned toward the running boy. His voice was flat and hard with anger.

43

"Stay out of my way, Murdoch. Get out of this field or I'll take this to *you* and you have my word for it." He waved the stick menacingly over his head.

Behind them at that moment there was a flurry of sound as the little pony drummed his front hoofs on the ground, then he went off at a flying run, pounded the length of the meadow and leaped cleanly over the five-foot stone wall into the Mc-Farlane garden. The crowd gasped at the sight. One moment the trembling small horse had been standing in the meadow, the next he had bolted and sailed out of view as neatly as a deer.

From the other side of the wall came a high female shriek, than a scutter of hoofs and the sound of trellises smashing and the bird bath tumbling. The pony, confused and trapped, was rampaging through the garden, trampling the flower beds and strawberry patches in a frantic search for a way out. Finally, he found the graveled walk at the side of the big McFarlane house and tore out the front gate and into the main street of Duneen.

Rob, Katie, McFarlane, the miners and a surging crowd of spectators had rushed from the meadow and rounded the house just in time to see the ginger horse take off at full sprint. The sheer speed of the animal and the sharp click of his hoofs on the cobbles sent the market crowds scattering. A startled farmer lost his footing and toppled a wheelbarrow of cabbages into the gutter. Another dropped the crate of chickens he carried on his head, sending the birds squawking and fluttering into the confusion. The tinker's horse, frightened by the noise, dashed off down the street, pulling the wagon behind him, with Mrs.

Thomas hanging on the reins. A pair of frightened sheep, tethered in the square, began to *baa-baa* as though their hearts would break.

Then someone bumped against the hardware store display, sending crockery and cookie jars through the plate glass window with a shattering crash. Old Granny Merkle threw her mushrooms over her head in panic, and ducked into the bakery, shrilling, "Earthquake, earthquake!" Children screamed and clung to their mothers. Down the street, McFarlane pounded, shouting and brandishing his stick. Some of the villagers, stepping out of the shops at the noise, never caught sight of the ginger horse at all, but stood in terror, thinking McFarlane had gone mad.

Ahead, the pony bucked and thrashed his way to freedom, leaving havoc in his path.

As the tiny, racing hoofs carried the animal as far as the Old Ram's Head, the swinging doors were flung open by a crowd of curious farmers, who stared in bewilderment, wiping the foam of ale from their chins.

"Stop the black-hearted beast!" McFarlane shouted at them, panting up the cobblestones. "Stop him, I say."

But the sight of a small Shetland outracing and outsmarting the great Mr. McFarlane was too much for the drinkers. Someone began to laugh. At first it was a solitary snicker but soon that grew into a general, outright guffaw at the sight of a grown man, and the owner of the Duneen coal mines, being made a fool of by one small, tired and frightened pony.

At the sound of the laughter, McFarlane stopped in his

tracks, his breath coming in short puffs, his face damp with perspiration. He could not bear to be laughed at, ever. Ahead of him, the ginger horse darted away, slipped behind a yew hedge and was gone from sight.

McFarlane tossed his stick into the gutter and turned to the three miners, still close by his side. "Get back to your work, all of you—whatever you should be doing," he ordered sullenly. "There'll be time enough tomorrow to take care of the beast...."

6

THE mood of the day suddenly darkened with Mr. McFarlane's threat and Rob felt his breath coming short and quick. At that moment, he couldn't tell whether it was from running or because Mr. McFarlane's last words had filled him with sharp fear. He signaled to Katie and the two children slipped back up the street and into the turmoil of the square.

"Let's pretend it's none of our business," Rob whispered. "Let's pretend we don't care."

With the coin in his pocket he bought a paper of fish-and-chips, getting a few pennies in change. The two children sat on a curbstone, quietly sharing their lunch. In front of the hardware store, the owner was sweeping up broken pottery and window glass, swinging the broom with angry strokes. The loose chickens had been recaptured and were tethered by their legs to a lamp post, still squawking and fluttering. Granny Merkle threw her black shawl over her head and went moaning and wailing to anyone who would listen that her beautiful mushrooms were ruined. Around the square, people stood in clusters, talking excitedly, complaining about damaged goods, bruised shins and a half-dozen other grudges. The entire village was in a resentful uproar. After all, it was McFarlane's pony that had caused the damage. Then, little by little, the noise began to die down.

"I think it's all right now," Rob said thoughtfully, jingling the pennies in his pocket. "We'll stop by the hardware store for a bit of rope. Then we'll look for the ginger horse ourselves, but we'll have to be careful about it."

"If we find him, what will you do?" Katie asked.

"We'll take him round to the Minister," Rob answered firmly. "He's the only man in town who isn't afraid of Mr. McFarlane."

"You'll not find the Minister in on a Saturday," Katie reminded him. "It's his day to go and visit the sick."

"Then we'll hide the horse till we've had time to think," Rob said, unwilling to admit even to Katie that he had no clear idea at all as to what he meant to do. "Most important is to find the pony before McFarlane does."

For an hour or more they searched, walking up each street in the village, peering over fences and behind hedges, calling softly for the pony in coaxing tones. The ginger horse was not there. He was not in the McFarlane meadow, he was not on the dusty road leading to the mines, he was not hidden among the big piles of coal at the railroad siding. He seemed to have disappeared without a trace.

"If the wee thing has taken off for the hills, we'll never find him before dark," Rob said wearily.

"But he was too tired to go far," Katie told him. "He was panting and all thirsty."

"The *brook*," Rob said. "You know how he liked the brook." The two children ran once more to the meadow where the stream flowed under the McFarlane fence, then through the grove of aspen behind the church and out toward the wilder fields of the valley. They walked along the twisting banks, going upstream, pushing aside bushes and kicking at the clumps of winter-dried grass. "Ginger, Ginger," Rob called softly. "It's us, wee Ginger. . . ." There was not a sound except the flowing of water and the whisper of a light wind shivering the leaves of the aspen trees.

The children pushed on, watching the ground for footprints. Now the brook widened and then flowed into several smaller streams, making a marsh land that softened and oozed under their feet. A marsh bird fluttered up from its ground nest with a rush of wings. And then, suddenly, Rob pointed ahead toward a thick clump of rushes, brown and dried, with the heavy black cattail tops swaying in the wind. "There's the pony!" he whispered.

The little horse was lying on his side. His ribs were still rising and falling with heavy breathing, but his head was erect and he peered at the children through a sweat-dampened mane. Rob fell on his knees and hugged the animal's head to his chest, rocking back and forth as if he were cradling a baby. "You poor wee thing," he said soothingly. "You didn't want to go back to the old mines, did you? You thought you were free."

The pony lay quiet, nuzzling at Rob's hand, seeming too exhausted to rise. Rob patted the animal's nose soothingly and said, "I've no carrot for you today, laddie. But I'll bring *two* tomorrow."

Katie shivered. "It's going to be dark soon," she said, "and my feet are wet. What are we going to do?"

Rob thought a moment. "We'll wait here until the sun goes down a bit more." He paused before continuing, "Then we'll lead the pony into the graveyard and tether him out of sight. Surely there will be no one there tonight. And we can talk to the Minister in the morning."

They waited quietly, shivering now from both chill and worry. . . . Finally, Rob took the length of rope from his sweater pocket and made a loop around the pony's neck, gently urging the tired animal to his feet. Already, the field beyond the brook was graying with dusk.

"We'll try it now," Rob said. "You go on ahead—up into the woods and over to the church. I'll follow with the ginger horse. If you see anyone, whistle and I'll stay quiet till all's clear."

Katie darted off and Rob listened as she brushed through the reeds and went into the meadow. Her footsteps faded among the trees and there was silence. He waited, counting slowly to ten, then set off himself for the churchyard, with the little pony jogging along tiredly behind until they had rejoined Katie.

The children tied one end of the rope firmly around the base of an old stone baptismal font, tucked up close to the shelter

of the church wall. About them, the tombstones and carved angels loomed big and dark, like silent people gathered together in the half-light. The little horse stood upright, but he was shivering so that his rough hide trembled under the boy's hand.

"He got all sweated and chilled from the long run and from fright," Rob said, his voice worried. Quickly he bent to unlace and slip off his boots. Then he peeled off his thick, hand-knitted wool socks. "We'd better give him a good rubdown," he said, handing Katie a rolled-up sock.

Working one on each side, the children rubbed down the pony briskly, the thick socks drying and then brushing like a currycomb. Soon the pony's shivering ceased. Last of all, Rob took off his good brown sweater and put it over the pony's back, tying the arms loosely under the neck, like a shawl.

Then the children slipped out of the graveyard and began to hurry for home, with Rob stepping carefully because the wet boots rubbed painfully on his bare feet. "Not a word now!" he whispered to Katie at her own gate.

Except for a little sputter of flame in the coal stove, the Murdoch house was dark. Rob's supper sat on a plate at the back of the stove. Mac was over at the Burns bakery and old Jock Murdoch had gone down to the Ram's Head for his Saturday night pint of ale.

Rob gave a sigh of weary relief. He could eat his supper in quiet and slip off to bed. No need to answer any questions about the day. And no need until tomorrow to worry about the ginger horse.

7

THE first church bells of the morning were like part of a dream, but a bad dream to Rob. He stirred in his sleep, muttered unhappily and then pulled the covers over his head. All Duneen slept a bit later on Sundays, with the first bells pealing out over the valley at seven sharp, to wake the parishioners for eight o'clock services. Rob tossed and dozed fitfully for a while longer.

It was Mac who roused him, shaking his shoulder gently. "Might as well wake up," he said. "You're having a bad time of it in your sleep."

Rob sat bolt upright, his mind racing at once to the ginger horse. "The time! What time is it?" he asked.

"You've time enough," his brother answered, squinting into the cloudy little mirror over the chest of drawers as he knotted his Sunday necktie. "It is no more than fifteen minutes to eight now. Father's walked on ahead and I'm stopping by for Margaret. Your porridge is on the stove."

Rob leaped from bed and ran into the back garden in his bare feet, splashed his face clean with the sharply cold water from the pump, then hurried to his bedroom to dress. He heard Mac close the front door and the house was quiet.

Rob's teeth were chattering and his hands fumbled so he could hardly button his shirt and pull on his rough tweed Sunday trousers. He had meant to get there first. He had meant to slip around to the back of the church, to see that the pony was hidden and safe before any of the villagers arrived for services. There was no time now for breakfast, no time to look for Katie. He knotted his boot laces firmly, brushed back his hair with his hand and rushed out the front door. His footsteps were loud on the cobblestones as he raced down the street, almost bowling over Granny Merkle as she tapped along with her cane on the way to church.

Although the bright spring morning was already lit with sun, there was a mood of cold sternness and tight-lipped disapproval among the parishioners clustered on the church steps. The ladies of the village were prim in their Sunday blacks, the men looked bulky and a bit ill-at-ease in white shirts and suit coats. Only the little children, with carefully brushed hair and neat, fresh clothes, seemed as carefree as usual. Rob knew something was wrong.

Jaimie Lauder, the butcher, who also served as vestryman, came around the corner of the old structure and said to the group, "The Minister asks that you all go inside and be seated.

We'll have services as usual—as soon as he settles the troubles out back."

Rob felt his mouth go dry. Quietly, trying not to attract attention, he slipped around the side of the church and up to the iron gate of the old graveyard. Inside stood the Minister, the McFarlanes and a half-dozen other villagers, staring, pointing and shaking their heads solemnly. For a moment, Rob could not believe his eyes. The old graveyard looked topsy-turvy, as if someone had turned it upside down and forgotten how to put it back in place.

The turf was torn up in chunks and the early daffodils, crocuses and other grave plantings had been pawed and pounded into the ground. One big stone angel rested flat on its back on the grass, its outstretched arms reaching up as if begging for help. A row of tombstones had been toppled, tearing up with them long, straggling strands of ivy that had grown over them with the years. The baptismal font lay on its side, a broken bit of tether rope still knotted around the base. Hoof prints marked the ground everywhere—but the ginger horse was nowhere in sight.

Above them, from the church tower, the eight o'clock chimes began to sound, the great iron clappers striking the bells with tones that vibrated and shook the air over the graveyard. In that instant, Rob knew what had happened. The first church bells had alarmed the pony and the continued loud ringing had worked the powerful little animal into a frenzy of fright. His struggles had broken the tether and pulled the baptismal font over against the stone angel. And when the angel fell it hit the first gravestone, toppling the others in the row like a falling house of cards. And then, evidently, the pony had fled. Now the last peal of the bells for services was echoing away.

"He's a devil, I tell you, stomping up the graves of Christians," Mr. McFarlane was shouting, shaking a fist at the devastation in the graveyard. "Not a pony at all but a ginger devil out to destroy the village and make a fool of me!"

The Minister put a hand on his arm. "You're steaming away like an old kettle that's got too hot," he said soothingly. "It's just a wee horse on the loose and no more than that, surely. I'll get some of the students to work out here tomorrow and we'll have the place as right as rain by noontime."

"And who is to go on paying the damages?" demanded McFarlane. "The broken shop windows, the vegetables ruined in the streets, the strawberry beds that took two years to grow? I'm not made of money and I'll not be made a fool of by something I own. . . ."

Suddenly, his loud, rough voice became low and thoughtful. "I have it now," he said. "I have it *now*. I'll put in a call for the county police to send over a constable from the town of Strathmoran this very afternoon. No, I'll drive over and fetch him myself. There'll be a reward for whoever finds the pony—and we'll have it shot on sight as a dangerous beast."

Rob grasped the gate until the sharp, cold iron almost cut into his hands. He bit his lip to keep from crying out.

"That's a foolish decision, Angus," the Minister said firmly. "Come in to services now. Perhaps you'll feel more kindly after you've prayed a bit."

"A man has no time for praying with this kind of business to attend to," McFarlane said and stomped off through the graveyard toward his own house, a bit of torn-up ivy catching and trailing around his ankle.

Rob slipped behind some bushes and the Minister and the others brushed past him on the way into church. Then he sank to the ground and sat with both hands pressed tightly over his face. He wanted to blot out the sight and thought of everything—his father's inevitable disapproval, McFarlane's raging anger, the picture of a Strathmoran constable with a shotgun. Saving the ginger horse was all that mattered. He was silent, barely breathing, while the organ music for the first hymn poured out the church windows.

*   *   *   *

About an hour later, Rob and the ginger horse had reached the mouth of the stream, just below the point where the water rushed from the mountain rock and began its flow down into the valley. Rob's boots were sodden and his rough tweed trousers stuck with twigs and burrs. The two had clung close to the river bank all the way, with Rob going ahead to push aside reeds and bushes, the pony trotting on behind at tether's end.

Without the pony, Rob could have cut out across the wide open meadow in front of the church, using familiar paths leading into the mountains, as he often did when he went to fish or climb the great, gray rocks. But today, even though he was convinced that Mr. McFarlane had set out for Strathmoran at once in his car, it was important not to be seen or followed.

Under cover of the organ music, he had slipped out of the churchyard and back to the brook, retracing steps and beating back the reeds to the nest-like hollow where the tired ginger horse had been lying only yesterday. The Shetland was not there. Rob whistled softly and called his name. Then he put his ear to the ground, listening for any movement that might sound above the ripple of the stream. Ahead of him there was a rustle in the tall, dried weeds. He advanced slowly—and there stood the little horse, calm and cocky now, browsing contentedly in the grass, the long tether dragging.

Rob knew that speed and secrecy were important to his new plan. No one but Katie knew he had found the pony yesterday. And no one but Katie knew he had tied it in the graveyard. She would never tell, he was sure. With McFarlane's reward in mind, the people of the village would be searching for the Shetland—but not for Rob. He had decided to lead the pony to a hiding place he knew in the mountains, a flat grassy area surrounded by high, scraggy rocks. Rob had played there often. There was running water and a good stretch of shrubs and grass. No one would find the ginger horse in this lonely spot. The constable with the shotgun would go back to Strathmoran. The mines would go back to full schedule on Monday, with the other pit ponies pulling coal carts through the dark tunnels. McFarlane would find other things to shout about. By Tuesday or Wednesday, the quiet village would be back to normal. Then, and only then, Rob decided as he plodded through the muddy brush of the banks, would he go to the Minister and tell him about the pony.

A white rush of water spurted from a gash in the mountainside, crashing down onto the rocks below. It was a narrow waterfall but gushed with a force that sent sprays of fine mist into the air. Rob half-circled around the falls and began climbing the rough, gray crags on one side. He looked back at the pony, leaping agilely behind him, the blond mane and heavy eyelashes beaded with drops of mountain water. Rob remembered what the Minister had said about Shetlands . . . "as sure-footed as goats and can find a bit of grass here, a bit of grass there. . . ." Rob's own stomach ached with hunger and he thought longingly of the bowl of porridge at the back of the stove, but the little pony gamboled behind him, well-fed and watered, without a care in the world.

The climb was steep and hard. To Rob, this was an unfamiliar path and his feet slipped often on loose stones, sending rattles of gravel down behind him. At last, he grasped a thick-stemmed bush and pulled himself up between two huge rocks into the sheltered plateau. The pony clattered behind him.

Rob rested a moment, puffing loudly. Then he tethered the Shetland to a scrubby fir tree, bent with years of wind, tying the rope in a secure knot. Nearby was a small, clear, pool made from a seepage in the rocks. Rob leaned on one of the big boulders, wind-worn and pitted with centuries of rain and snow. Far below him, across the smooth April-green of the meadows, he could see Duneen, looking like a peaceful toy village sprawled out in the distance. There seemed to be a light haze over the town, as if every kitchen stove was sending up smoke from the roast mutton or lamb stew of a Sunday dinner.

Rob sighed and lay on his back, folding his arms behind his head. He knew he had to return, and soon, but he wanted just a few more moments in the peace and silence of the mountains, with the ginger horse grazing safely beside him. His eyes followed the rim of the mountains, the gray rocks he knew so well. Already, the crags were spotted with the white of snowdrops, the hollows tinged faintly purple with new spring heather. Some distance beyond, the mountain rock was of a blacker color, rougher and more unfriendly. And far beyond that, Rob knew, out past the tunnel where the little train chugged through, was another valley. The children never played or explored in the black rocks. They had been warned never to do this. That ridge of the mountains was too far from home and too dangerously honeycombed with crevasses and twisting, narrow caves.

It was windy, as it almost always was in the mountains, a singing wind that whistled between rocks and made the bushes twang and hum like the strings of old harps. Above, the sky was a clear blue but scudding with white clouds. Rob had always loved to watch the skies in the mountains, whether clear or dark and rumbling with storm. Looking into the sky, feeling its vast majesty, always made him feel very close to his brother David, almost as if he had known him and could talk to him. And he always felt proud and awed that his own brother had flown through that sky.

I'm daydreaming again, Rob thought to himself. I'm daydreaming when I should be hurrying home so Father doesn't miss me at noontime dinner. He fixed his eyes on one small, hurrying cloud. I'll lie here, he thought, just till that one gets blown out of sight. Then I'll start the climb down.

* * * *

At the top of his own street, Rob stopped to wipe at the mud on his boots with a pocket handkerchief. Then he plucked the burrs from his trousers. His hands were dirty and scratched from the rough climb and, for the first time, he noticed a sharp, stinging cut on the back of his knuckles. Then he looked up at the sky and took a deep breath, hoping the good air would clear his head and lift the heavy burden of worry that hung over his thoughts. The ginger horse was safe. And he would be safe, once he reached his own home.

But when Rob opened the front door, the Murdoch kitchen-sitting room looked smaller than he ever remembered, as if the walls had been pushed in until there was barely room to breathe. Four men sat facing him, stiff and stern in the straight-backed wooden chairs. Jock Murdoch and his son Mac were at either side of the kitchen table. Angus McFarlane was in a chair by the window, with the constable from Strathmoran at his side, a small, soft-faced man in a green leather hunting jacket, a shotgun—on safe—cradled comfortably in one arm.

Rob stopped short. "You've not fooled anyone, you young rascal," said Mr. McFarlane in a quiet, self-satisfied voice. Then he held up Rob's good brown sweater, the one he had tied around the pony's neck, and the short bit of tether that had been knotted around the baptismal font.

McFarlane waved the sweater like a triumphal flag. "Granny

63

Merkle found *this* in the graveyard," he announced.

"*Granny Merkle?*" Rob echoed, his voice small.

"That dotty creature is always puttering around the tombstones, visiting old friends. At her age, she's got more friends below ground than she has in the village," McFarlane explained. "And *this*," he continued, holding up the tether, "I spotted this myself and it didn't take much asking to find out who bought a new rope at the hardware shop just yesterday."

"I think you've done something you shouldn't, lad," Rob's father said, his weathered face looking tired and sad. "Can you not tell Mr. McFarlane what you've done with the wee pony?"

Rob stared down at his boots, glad he had wiped off the mud from the climb. Now they could only guess at where he'd been. In his mind's eye, he could see the ginger horse, high on the mountain, hidden from harm, the free wind blowing through his mane. The boy said nothing.

McFarlane began to speak in a shrewdly reasonable tone. "I can understand how a boy might feel about an animal. I used to keep rabbits myself in the old days. Even had a pigeon once that wouldn't eat unless I fed it on the window sill." For a moment his voice seemed almost kind. Then his eyes hardened. "But what I can't understand is a boy with a good Christian upbringing not knowing the difference between right and wrong! The fact is, property is property, whether it's animal, vegetable or mineral. That's my horse and it belongs to me. And I demand that you tell me where you've hidden my property!" He was standing now, towering over Rob and almost seeming to fill the room with his bulk and the blackness of his

anger. Rob was overwhelmed by the power and authority of the big man. His mind seemed to be blanked with panic. He could not even make himself consider whether McFarlane was right or wrong. But he knew he could not betray the ginger horse. The room was so quiet that even the gentle flickering of the flame in the stove seemed loud and ominous.

It was Mac who broke the silence, rising to come over and put his arm around his brother's shoulders. "Property *is* property, Mr. McFarlane. I'll agree with you there. But sometimes property changes hands. I've thought of a way that you can *have* your rights. I've a bit of money put by. Let me buy the pony from you. Tell me what you think it's worth and I'll pay you for the life of the animal." Rob pushed both hands deep into his trouser pockets to keep them from trembling.

McFarlane turned to Mac and stared in seeming disbelief. "Have you no shame in you? A grown man aiding and backing a boy who is defying his elders, sneaking and thieving behind their backs?"

Then he shook a menacing finger at Jock Murdoch. "And you. What do you say to the fact that you've raised a son who's a *liar* and a *thief?*"

Jock Murdoch stood, squared his thick shoulders and said, "Angus McFarlane, we've been friends together in this village for more years than I can count. I've worked for you. I've answered your beck and call. But you'll not call anyone a liar and a thief in my house—not today or till the longest day you live!"

McFarlane looked at the wall over Jock Murdoch's head, not

66

wanting to meet the miner's eyes. His voice was tight and deep, like a man so upset he wanted to shout, but the words were quiet and cold. "I'm telling the lad, and I'm telling him in front of you. He has until morning to return my pony. The constable will stay at my house until then. And there will not be a Murdoch, father or son, who will get work in my mines till the pony is back in my hands."

Then he stalked to the front door. The constable, looking ill at ease, nodded a good-by to Jock Murdock and followed behind.

8

IT WAS a bleak afternoon for the Murdochs. Mac put on the kettle for tea and put out wheat bread and the honey pot. For a while, the whistle of the kettle was the only sound in the house. At the table, Rob was unable to eat but sat cupping the mug of hot tea in his hands, trying to get warmth back into fingers that felt numb and cold.

Finally, Jock Murdoch began to talk in his gruff, halting way, his eyes on the boy's face. "I knew you'd gone daft on the horse," he said kindly. "It's all you've talked about all week. Giving it carrots and everything. You've needed something to love, brought up in a house without a mother to want you and care for you." He paused, thoughtfully stirring his tea.

"And I know I'm not much good for fun, either," Rob's father said, sadly. "I'm an old man to you. I feel old to myself sometimes. But I know what's right and what's wrong. I know there is a normal and natural order to life—a straight road. I've worked year after year in the mines and I believe that's part of God's order. I *took* my responsibility, my way in life. And the pony has a purpose and a responsibility, too."

Rob said respectfully, "I don't understand you, Father."

The older man looked cheered. These were the first words Rob had spoken since McFarlane left the house. "I never was good with words," he said, pushing the honeypot and bread closer to Rob. "Let's look at it this way. Think it over for yourself." His voice was almost jovial. "What would the world be like, Robbie, if Mac didn't go down into the mines and if I stopped going into the mines and if everyone stopped what they were doing just because they didn't *like* it? Many is the time that a man *has* to do things that aren't just to his fancy."

But, Rob thought to himself, some men find ways to do things that make them feel happy and free. Sometimes there is a spirit that wants to live life in a different fashion. David had that spirit, and even his death couldn't change the fact that he had a special courage, had met life as an exciting challenge. . . .

"You're shivering, lad," he heard his father say. "Get undressed and get into your bed. I'll bring your tea. You look chilled and like you're coming down with something. Don't fret any more today. You can go out in the morning and bring the horse back where it belongs."

Rob sipped his tea with the bedcovers tight around his shoulders. Then he lay down and turned his face to the wall. Twice during the long afternoon he heard his father tiptoe to look in the door. He pretended to be asleep. And then he must really have slept, because he woke to see the gray dusk of twilight outside the window. He was cold and unhappy and the bed-clothes seemed heavy on his body. He sighed, thought of the pony tethered up among the rocks, a small, warm living thing, still safe. And then he willed himself to fall asleep once more....

It was nearly midnight when the boy woke again, roused by the creak of springs as Mac lowered himself into his own bed. "You're awake?" Mac whispered.

"Yes," answered Rob.

"No wonder," his brother said. "McFarlane's rantings would give anyone nightmares."

"You were good to offer to buy the pony," Rob said simply.

"I have some money," Mac explained. "I've saved a bit here and a bit there—for Margaret and me. And I've gotten good at my drafting. I like that work. Someday we'll make a try for it in Edinburgh."

Rob swallowed hard and then said, "But you'll not have much money to save if McFarlane won't let you work in the mines."

Mac laughed and thumped his pillow into shape with his fist. "Old penny-pinching McFarlane? Do you think he'd lay off two of his best men for a grudge? No, we'll be back on the first shift in the morning, as always."

"And the pony?" Rob asked.

Mac was silent for a moment and then answered gravely, "That's up to you, Rob. A man has to make certain decisions for himself."

"The ginger horse doesn't want to go back to the mines,"

Rob said urgently, desperate for someone to understand what he felt. "You saw that. He wants a chance to run free. . . ."

Mac's voice was low. "I've wanted to run myself," he said, "many a time. But I can't seem to make it over that first bit of fence."

Rob lay stiff and silent in his bed, fists clenched at his sides, his heart pounding with the excitement of his decision. He had a few hours to wait but he knew now, exactly and clearly, what he was going to do.

*   *   *   *

The waiting seemed endless. . . . Finally, Rob rose, dressing swiftly and quietly in the darkened bedroom. Then he took the old clock from atop the chest of drawers and tiptoed into the kitchen. He held the clock close to the faint, glowing light from the coal stove. The hands stood exactly at five o'clock.

Outside, Rob walked softly so his steps made no sound in the street. At the McBain house, he remembered the squeaking gate and opened it carefully, an inch at a time. Then he crept around to tap lightly on Katie's window. In the dimness, he saw her sit up in bed, look startled for a moment, then reach out to tap a return signal on the inside windowpane.

Rob waited in the shadows, each second seeming to stretch into minutes, until he heard her step softly from the front door. He put his finger to his lips and whispered, "Come quickly. Don't talk. We're going to free the wee pony now—and forever."

Katie looked puzzled, her face still soft with sleep, her thick ribboned braid all fuzzed and untidy from the pillow. "But whatever can you—" she began.

"Not now," Rob broke in impatiently. "Someone might hear. I'll explain everything outside the village."

The two children walked cautiously through the quiet streets, sticking close to hedges and fences, stopping every time a dog barked, alerted to any sound that might come from behind shuttered windows. As they passed the McFarlane house, big and brooding in the pre-dawn light, they scarcely dared to breathe. Next, they slipped by the church and out onto the broad, open meadows beyond the village. At that moment, both children broke into a run, darting ahead like shadows, black on black, into the thin morning light. The grass was wet with dew and rough weeds whipped and tore at their ankles as they ran. They had made this journey through the meadows and into the mountains so often in daylight that now their feet followed familiar paths out of habit. But this time both were nervous and afraid. The sky had begun to lighten to a pearly-gray. Early morning swirls of mist clung and eddied over the ground. It was like running pell-mell through a frightening dream.

Suddenly, behind them and from the shadow of the church, a group of men stepped out, faces grave, voices silent. It was Angus McFarlane, the constable from Strathmoran and a couple of miners. McFarlane, shrewd and determined, had suspected that Rob might slip off to the pony's hiding place before daybreak, so he had been waiting and watching. Silently, with unlit flashlights, the men began to stalk the children across the meadow. Ahead, the running footsteps echoed in the morning stillness, distinct and easy to follow.

At that moment, McFarlane was joined by a swift, dark figure from the church. It was the Minister, his black coat buttoned tight around his throat against the morning chill. "As a man of God, I am glad you have joined us to see that the Right is done," McFarlane said in a pious whisper.

"I'm joining you because you're behaving like a man gone out of his senses," the Minister replied curtly. "You think you're trying to save your blasted pony. It's the children I'm out to keep from harm."

Farther ahead, Katie and Rob raced toward the mountains, hope rising in their hearts as they felt the first rough rocks of the slopes beneath their feet. "We're going to make it!" Rob cried triumphantly as he waited for Katie to catch up with him. Looking back at the village, he saw no lights, heard no sounds. Behind him, the meadow seemed shrouded in silence and fog.

Impatient now, the children began the steep climb, watching alertly for landmarks—tall trees, craggy rocks—that began to loom clear through the morning light. Rob scrambled on ahead, pausing now and then to check that Katie was safely behind him. At last, in a state of exhaustion and joy, the pair reached the grassy hollow, circled by concealing crags and boulders. The ginger pony was there, still tethered and safe. He nuzzled their hands with recognition, whinnying softly. Both children hugged the little horse, feeling the warmth from his hard-muscled, vigorous body driving the chill from their own.

"I knew you'd hidden him yesterday," Katie whispered, still feeling fearful in the half-light of dawn. "I didn't know you'd thought of this place."

"But he can't *stay* here," Rob told her excitedly. "He can't stay here forever. We've got to put him where Mr. McFarlane will never find him. We've got to set him really free!"

"Where?" Katie asked.

Rob's voice was grave and determined. "I'm going to lead the pony up over the black rocks. I'm going to take him up to the pass near the railroad tunnel and turn him loose in the next valley. . . . Don't you see, Katie," he went on. "It's like putting him into a new world. He'd have the run of the whole valley and the mountains on the other side. It's spring now and all of summer lies ahead. He'll find plenty to eat and drink. A Shetland can take care of itself. The Minister told you that. Maybe some farmer over there might find him. The pony would like to be on a farm. And he'd be free of the mines, free of Mr. McFarlane!"

Katie's voice was troubled. "We've been told many a time not to climb on the black rocks."

"I mean to take the pony up myself," Rob said firmly, untying the tether from the fir tree.

Katie hesitated just a moment. "I'll climb with you halfway," she decided. "And then wait for you to come back down."

Around them, the crests of the mountains were now clearly touched by the pink of dawn. Shrubs and pine trees were taking shape in the light. Ahead and above them, they could see the narrow cleft in the black rocks through which the pony would be set free into the valley beyond.

They started single file, Rob first, then the pony, with Katie struggling along behind. Both children were silent, concentrating on the slippery paths and rough rocks beneath their feet. Soon they left the grassy, moss-chinked trails and began the slower climb on the black rocks themselves. This part of the mountains looked as if some giant fire had charred it centuries ago, leaving the stone darkened, split and barren of all plant life.

Rob paused, looking about him, uncertain just how to go ahead. Then he chose a narrow, natural path, winding upward along the face of a high shaft of rock, a mountain wall pitted and marred with great hollows. The little horse jumped along nimbly but the children climbed with caution, testing the ground before each step. Rocks slipped beneath their feet, rattling and scuttling off the side of the path. Little by little, they were making their way up toward the pass.

"I've got to rest. Just a few moments," Katie pleaded. Rob stopped and they both leaned against the mountain, breathing deeply, feeling the freshness of the breeze on their hot cheeks.

Suddenly, from below them but not far away, there was a distinct scutter of falling rocks and a bitter voice saying, "Blast that devil pony! A man could break a leg climbing in these mountains."

Teetering on the edge of the path, Rob looked down. Through a screen of bushes, he could just glimpse a knot of men toiling up the trail behind them, flashlights bobbing to light the ground. In the half-light he could not recognize them, but he knew that dreaded voice. He and Katie were being followed by

Angus McFarlane! The thought chilled him to the spine. The boy looked up at the narrow pass in the high black rocks, so very near and yet too far now to reach without being seen.

"Quick, Katie, quick!" he urged, at the same time jerking at the tether so the pony jumped after him. Up they scrambled, heedless of the noise in their panic, kicking showers of rocks down the mountainside. Suddenly, at one side of the trail, Rob saw an opening in the rocks, a dark, narrow split, just barely wide enough for a child to slip into. "Here," he said. "Here, Katie. We'll hide in this cave so they'll think they've lost us."

He stepped in first, using one hand to guide himself along the wall of the cave, with the pony close behind. Katie stepped just inside the opening. "Further in," Rob urged. "They'll see you there for sure." And he inched his way deeper into the mountain. He looked back. The little slit of light through which they had entered still seemed too close for safety.

"We've got to keep out of sight till they go away," Rob said urgently. "We'll go in just a bit deeper, where they can't possibly see us or hear us. There are a dozen caves up here. They'll not know where to look."

Cautiously, he stepped deeper into the narrow cave, touching the wall carefully with his fingertips as he moved, trying to memorize a path on the stone. Abruptly, that wall ended and the passageway made a sharp corner turn. The children and the pony stepped around the corner. They were shut off completely from the outdoor light.

"We're safe now," Rob said, blinking to try to accustom his eyes to the darkness. "Just don't say a word."

"I don't want to stay here too long," Katie whispered. "I don't like the dark."

"Just a few moments. Just till we're sure they've gone away," Rob assured her.

Both children were silent then. Between them, the little pony breathed easily and softly. From a distance, there seemed to come the sound of voices and heavy footsteps, but the atmosphere of the cave had a muffling quality and Rob was not sure he heard anything. A single drop of water splashed down on his cheek from somewhere far above. Beneath his feet, the floor of the cave felt slippery and insecure, so he moved a little farther into the darkness, trying to find a firmer place on which to stand. Katie and the ginger horse were close behind.

Again there was a noise and Rob strained his ears to make out what it was and from where it came. There seemed to be echoes of distant shouts . . . then there was silence. After that, he heard another sound, a frightening bubbling gurgle, like water spouting in the unknown darkness. There was a strange smell in the cavern, a smell of damp, musty age and clammy rock. He was so eager to get back into the familiar daylight that every second seemed to tick loud in his head, like an angry clock. But he still could not be sure that McFarlane and the constable were not waiting for them, one posted on each side of the cave entrance. He willed himself to keep silent, shifting about a little to warm up his damp feet.

In the darkness, he reached out until he touched Katie's hand. "Come stand by me," he said. "We'll be warmer close together." Carefully, she pushed past the little pony and stood at his side. He could feel her shivering. "We'll be out of here soon," he said reassuringly and then shuddered himself as he heard those words resounding in faint, whispery echoes through the darkness.

"Let's each count to five hundred in our heads," Katie said urgently. "And then we'll go back out."

They counted in silence. "Five hundred!" she announced quickly.

"Three hundred and seventy-five, three hundred and seventy-six," Rob said disapprovingly and then counted on until he had reached five hundred. He took a deep breath, "*Now* we go! Take my shirt tail and hang on," he instructed Katie, and, shifting the pony's tether to his right hand, he began to feel along the wall with his left, trying to remember just how the rock had been patterned as they crept into the cave. The children moved slowly, staring ahead hopefully for the little quarter moon of light that would mark the entrance into which they had stepped. Their feet shuffled along the damp floorway of the cave. The pony ticktacked behind them.

Rob felt his heart pound until his ribs ached. He blinked and blinked his eyes, hoping to clear away some of the darkness. The dusk of the cave seemed to be crowding in, touching his face with black feathers.

It was Katie who spoke first. "Rob, Rob," she said breathlessly, "we didn't walk this far coming in."

"We're nearly there now," he answered, rubbing his hand desperately along the cave wall. This surface seemed different from the first rock he had touched. That had been coarse and

pitted. Now the cave was made up of ridged layers of stone, running sideways in strips along the wall. He came to no abrupt corner such as he had felt on the way in. Instead, the wall seemed to be curving away and the rock was almost soft and crumbling to the touch.

"Let's back up and start again," he suggested. They backed up along the passageway and then started forward again. But they saw no light, found no opening. In the darkness, all sense of direction seemed to be gone. Around them, they sensed the solid, centuries-old bulk of the mountain. They were hopelessly lost.

Katie began to cry, her sobs soft and breathy in the close air. "We've got to keep trying," Rob said firmly, shuffling ahead. The cave passageway twisted and turned. At one point, the floor became wet and rock-loose beneath their feet. Again, they backed up and tried another passageway.

Neither child had any idea as to how long they crept on and on in the smothering darkness. Their hearts tight with fear, all sense of time was lost. At one point, they scurried hopefully toward a shaft of light, only to find it came from a small split in the rocks, high, high over their heads. They stood helpless, gazing at the pinpoint of sky so far above them, shouting and shouting for help. There was no answer, only the scared, rocking echoes of their own voices coming back at them from a hundred different caverns and passageways.

Finally, the cave seemed to widen into a room, loud with the sound of flowing water. The children sank onto the cold rock, huddled together in a paralysis of fright, too terrified to go further, too bewildered to pick a route back. The ginger pony stood behind them, patient at the end of the tether.

"Have we been in the cave long?" Katie asked, her voice trembling.

"Not too long," Rob answered, trying to make his own voice confident and firm. But he actually did not know whether they had been in there ten minutes or two hours. In the darkness, he could remember nothing clearly about the directions taken or the twists and turns they'd followed. But almost as if he were hearing voices, he did remember the many warnings given to all the children of Duneen about the dangers of the black rocks, with their near-bottomless crevasses and treacherous caves.

"Do you think Mr. McFarlane and the men thought we'd gone back to the village?" Katie asked fearfully. "Do you think they've gone back themselves?"

Rob shrugged in the darkness. He simply did not know. And he had the dreadful, sinking conviction that he and Katie would not get out of the heart of the mountain alive. He tried hard not to panic, biting his lip and grasping at the rock on which he sat until the tips of his fingers were scraped and bloody.

Beside him, Katie's voice was strangely small and faint. "I don't think I can breathe anymore, Robbie," she said. "I can't breathe right."

Rob took a deep breath but fright had made his own lungs feel strained and aching. He stood up carefully and stepped over to the ginger horse. In the darkness, he put his two hands on the pony's ribs, feeling them rise and fall evenly. Then he put a hand in front of the muzzle. The breath came warm and regular on his palm.

"The air is good, Katie," he said. "You're feeling faint because you're frightened, as you've every reason to be. But the pony's breathing just right."

"It's easy for him," she said, almost bitterly. "He's used to tunnels and darkness. I'm afraid. He's spent all his life trekking through the black coal mines—"

Rob hugged the little pony's head so roughly and abruptly that it whinnied in surprise. "That's it! That's it, Katie! He'll do it for us!" Rob heard his excited voice echo crazily in the darkness.

"We need a longer rope," he said. "Give me your hair ribbons, give me your stockings—but quick, quick!" He fumbled to untie the rope from around the pony's neck. Katie twisted the ribbons out of her braid, her hair falling loose around her shoulders. Then she took off her long tan stockings. Working clumsily in the dark, Rob tied them all together, lengthening out the tether.

"We need something thick and harder, something for a mouth bit." In the blackness, he heard a tearing sound and Katie handed him a large strip of the hand-tatted lace from the hem of her petticoat.

Rob's voice was almost fierce with excitement and hope. "Get behind me, Katie," he ordered, "and hold onto my shirt for your life."

Grasping the pony by the mane, Rob guided him until he stood directly ahead in the cave. With trembling hands, he tied the wad of coarse lace in the middle of the rope, then put it into the pony's mouth as a bit. Next he laid the makeshift harness of rope, stockings and ribbon back over the animal's shoulders, holding the ends firmly in his own hands. The little animal stood docile and quiet.

Rob's next words rang out like a fervent petition. *"Gee on, laddie! Gee on with you, Ginger!"* He knew that this same command was given to pit ponies every day, down in the darkness of the Duneen coal mines.

After a moment's hesitation, the ginger horse moved forward, with the children stepping carefully behind him. This was no longer the freedom-wild pony that had skittered over the pasture, kicked up flower gardens and jumped a five-foot wall. This was a working animal, plodding with the steady, slow *clip-clop* of pit ponies in the mines, judging the ground with cautious hoofs, moving methodically and instinctively toward the outside world. His ears were laid back as he listened to the sounds of underground trickles and loose rocks. His eyes, with their long sandy lashes, peered out intently, accustomed by long habit to seeing in the near-dark.

Once he stopped abruptly, refusing to move, as the sound of falling stones indicated that this bend of the path led to the edge of a deep crevass. He turned, picked another route and then a third, always with the methodical surefooted plod of the experienced pit pony. As time dragged on in an infinity of fear, the children became too exhausted to do anything but trudge along behind.

And then suddenly, through the cave, there came the faintest sound of a human voice. "We're here! We're here!" Rob shouted in response and his voice echoed back from a dozen chambers. Outside, men shouted in answer but their words splintered off in a confusion of directions. Rob tried to change Ginger's course, to point him straight in the direction from which he thought the voices sounded but the pony came to a stubborn dead stop. Again his ears went flat. Regardless of the many echoes, the pit pony chose his own path.

The children followed in tense silence, hope and despair mounting side by side. Then they came to an abrupt turn in the narrow passageway and saw a flashlight of the miners, signaling and searching, just outside the mouth of the cave. The ginger horse quickened his steps and trotted out into the clear mountain sunlight.

Behind him, Rob and Katie burst from the narrow cave opening and stopped short in the glare of daylight. For a moment, Rob's eyes seemed blinded. Then he saw the two miners, the great bulk of McFarlane and the weary constable from Strathmoran, his shotgun still in his hand. A few feet away, scrambling up the path, came the Minister, Jock Murdoch and Mrs. McBain, a heavy enveloping shawl thrown over her nightclothes, tears shining on her pretty face. Katie dashed to her mother and was greeted by a fresh shower of tears.

As his blinking eyes took in the scene, Rob saw McFarlane's big hand go out to grasp the makeshift bridle that held the little pony. He ran to his father and threw himself against the broad chest.

"Tell him, Dada," he shouted frantically. "Tell him I'll go into the mines *myself* if he'll let the ginger horse go free! I was taking him up to the pass in the black rocks. He could have run free in the next valley. . . ."

Jock Murdoch was hugging his son with one arm, pounding him gently on the back with his free hand, like someone comforting a colicky baby. His eyes were on the face of Boss McFarlane, haggard now and pale with the ashen grayness of pure fear.

"Tell him now, Dada," Rob urged. "Oh, please. I'll do anything he says!"

McFarlane said not a word to Rob. He was looking at Jock Murdoch and speaking directly to him. "I was wrong, Jocko," he said, saddened and humbled. "Before God, I know I've been wrong. I know now it's not all lads that can dance to the same tune."

The big man slipped the harness off the little Shetland and stood looking gratefully at the fragile arrangement of stockings, rope and bright hair ribbon. Then he struck the animal a sharp, brisk crack on the withers. The ginger horse started up, then lifted its hoofs in a skitter of speed and bolted up over the rocks and toward the rim of the mountains. Behind him, the full blond tail streamed like a plume.

"Away with you, you wee ginger devil!" McFarlane called out, but not loudly enough. The pony was already lost to sight beyond the pass in the black rocks.

9

THE kitchen window was open to let the warm, scented air of a May evening into the room. On a corner of the table stood a blue plate with a large slice of wedding cake, the frosting dotted with candy bows and roses. Jock Murdoch covered it with a clean dishtowel. "Might as well share that piece with our tea," he said.

"It was a good wedding, wasn't it, Father?" Rob asked eagerly.

"It was a good wedding," the old man said with finality and then took the kettle from the stove out to the garden pump to fill it with water.

Margaret Burns and Mac Murdoch had been married in the village church that afternoon, just one month after the ginger horse had left the valley. The Minister had read out the banns for three Sundays in a row and Mrs. McBain had gotten to work on a wedding dress. The veil was her own gift to the bride, a mist of tucked and flowing netting, put together miraculously by the seamstress out of a pair of white lace parlor curtains and yards of satin baby ribbon. "They'll be needing all the money they've saved," she told Rob, "to get themselves settled in Edinburgh."

The whole village came to the wedding. The McFarlanes had sat in a front pew and Mrs. McFarlane, in a great straw hat covered with pink satin roses, had sniffled and cried and made more noise than the mother of the bride. And because the Burns family were proud of their skill as bakers, and because their beloved Margaret was leaving the village, the wedding cake was three tiers high, the fanciest ever seen in Duneen.

There was sadness but there were no tears as both families waved good-by to the young Mac Murdochs, chugging off to a new life in Edinburgh on the afternoon train. But a strange, bitter-sweet loneliness crept into the Murdoch house with the coming of evening.

Rob went into his bedroom to get his schoolbooks. Even with the excitement of the pony and the wedding, there was still studying to be done, for summer vacation was weeks away. On an impulse, the boy fell to his knees and opened the bottom drawer of the chest. Carefully, he unwrapped the picture of his brother David, dusting the glass with his hand. The face looked back, bright-eyed and young. It seemed the right time.

When his father came in from the pump, Rob was bent over

his books at the kitchen table. Brother David was looking out of his picture frame on a nearby shelf, at home in his own kitchen for the first time in years.

Jock Murdoch set the kettle on the flame with a sharp thump. "You did that?" he asked sharply, pointing at the picture.

Rob nodded, a little afraid. "I thought, Father, we might not miss Mac so much if our David was back in the house."

The older man said nothing, but turned his back abruptly and began puttering with the tea things, setting out cups, plates, and a small pitcher of milk. Rob kept his eyes on his reading.

Finally, his father sat opposite him and began leafing through a history book. Now and then he paused, looking at the pictures, humming softly. The kettle on the stove began to hiss gently with steam.

Jock Murdoch shaded his eyes, squinting down at the words. "I just might have a bit of a read myself one of these days," he said, half to himself.

"Would you like to read these books? Would you like me to teach you to read?" Rob asked eagerly.

"It wasn't books I was thinking of reading," his father said. "But a man ought to be able to read letters from his own sons when they leave the valley."

Rob felt suddenly shy, like a small child caught with a stranger. "You know that I'll be here with you for a long, long time, Father," he said softly.

The kettle gave out a sharp whistle and the old man rose to make the tea. "But some day," he said, "some day, Rob— You're a lot more like that wild wee ginger horse than you know."

Outside, the stray tom cat jumped onto the window sill, meowing loudly and pawing at the fluttering curtain. Jock Murdoch looked up at the cat.

"Let him in, Rob. Let him in," he said gruffly. And then he laughed and brushed at his face with the back of his hand, as if he had laughed tears into his eyes. "It's not every cat in the village that's going to have a bit of wedding cake for its Saturday tea."

MAUREEN DALY

was born in County Tyrone, Northern Ireland, and grew up in Fond du Lac, Wisconsin. She first won literary distinction when she was fifteen, with a short story entitled *Fifteen*, which placed fourth in a national short story contest. The next year she won first place with a story called *Sixteen*, which was selected for the annual O. Henry Memorial Award volume. Her first novel, *Seventeenth Summer*, won the Dodd, Mead Intercollegiate Literary Fellowship contest and quickly became a best seller. She has never stopped writing since—writing vigorously, simply, and always with a new appeal.

Her articles and short stories have appeared in many national magazines, and, as a reporter-columnist for the *Chicago Tribune*, and, later, as associate editor of *Ladies' Home Journal* and consultant to the editors of the *Saturday Evening Post*, Miss Daly toured the United States, writing about and observing the American scene. *Mention My Name in Mombasa*, written with her husband, William P. McGivern, and her *Spanish Runabout* are fresh, spirited reports of visits to Europe and Africa.

Seventeenth Summer is currently in preparation for movie production by Warner Brothers, and *The Ginger Horse* will be seen as a Walt Disney television presentation.